THIS LITTLE PIGGY
WENT TO PRADA

Acknowledgements

Saint James Lohan for getting it, getting on with it, getting sufficiently in-touch with his feminine side to appreciate the difference between Manolo and Jimmy, Graff and Cartier and last but not least, getting it all done;

Master matchmaker Tamara Heber-Percy for introducing Piggy to Spy and perhaps, one day, you to the great love of your life;

Alison Lester who understands pease pudding, punctuation and just about everything I throw at her;

Angelynn Tan for bravely and patiently attempting to translate my hallucinogenic and baby-boggled mind onto paper;

Merissa Walker for understanding the mush of me and therefore the distinction between taupe, café latte and nude;

Adriana Ennab — the most indiscriminate, fickle, fanciful and forceful shopping companion a girl could wish for, a great friend and a great mother without ever resorting to rainbow sprinkles;

Jasmine Tan for keeping my feet on the ground and letting me rant and rave;

Mette and JMcG for, once upon a time, presenting me with a basket of black-and-white baby accessories and therefore giving me hope;

Zebby for taking it all on board and creatively spilling coffee over every page;

Howie for indulging all aspects of my diligent and thorough research and for 39 carats — still in debit;

Memememe without whom I would never have had to relate to cows jumping over the moon...

Thanks also to the team at Spy

Andrew Grahame — eye, ears and edit extraordinaire;

passionate Edward Orr — the rhyming financial controller who was quite possibly Edward Lear in his last life;

Aline Keuroghlian for just about everything in between and for taking me seriously

and the design team at Bloom

Oona Bannon for managing the design and attempting to speak Korean;

Jason Badrock for being clever and cleverly creative and being patiently receptive to my kooky ideas;

Cluny Brown for her expert organisational skills;

Graham at Trichrom for putting ink to paper

and

Kirsten McNally at Brand Couture for her invaluable advice and media guidance;

Sally Colwell and Rosie Jordan at Save the Children for their support and ours of them

THIS LITTLE PIGGY
WENT TO PRADA

BY

AMY ALLEN

NURSERY RHYMES FOR THE BLAHNIK BRIGADE

ILLUSTRATED BY EUN-KYUNG KANG

HarperEntertainment
An Imprint of HarperCollins*Publishers*

This book was originally published in Great Britain in 2005 by Spy Publishing.

Spy Publishing
192-194 Clapham High Street
London
SW4 7UD
United Kingdom

HarperCollins books may be purchased for educational, business, or sales promotional use. For information please write: Special Markets Department, HarperCollins Publishers, 10 East 53rd Street, New York, NY 10022.

First U.S. edition

ISBN-13: 978-0-06-113885-0
ISBN-10: 0-06-113885-1

06 07 08 09 10 TP 10 9 8 7 6 5 4 3 2 1

Contents

❋ THIS LITTLE PIGGY WENT TO PRADA,
THIS LITTLE PIGGY WENT TO CANNES. ❋
❋ THIS LITTLE PIGGY DINED AT NOBU,
AND THIS LITTLE PIGGY, HAKKASAN. ❋
❋ AND THIS LITTLE PIGGY WENT "WEE WEE WEE WEE!"
ALL THE WAY HOME BECAUSE SHE HAD A FAT BOTTOM! ❋

※ I HAD A LITTLE SHOE TREE, NOTHING WOULD IT BEAR
BUT MANOLO BLAHNIKS AND VINTAGE TAITTINGER. ※
※ THE QUEEN OF STYLE, MS WINTOUR, CAME TO SEE ME
AND WROTE A PIECE IN VOGUE ABOUT MY SHOE TREE. ※

✳ IF YOU'RE HAPPY AND YOU KNOW IT,
DO A POO! ✳
✳ IF THE MILK TASTES KIND OF FUNNY,
IT'S 'CHAMPOO'; ✳
✳ AT LEAST IT'S NOT SPUMANTE,
MUMMY'S TASTE IS RATHER FANCY, ✳
✳ IT WAS BOLLY, KRUG AND ONLY
PREMIER CRU! ✳

✳ Row row

❋ FRONT ROW FOR THE SHOW,
WITH THE HARPERS TEAM. ❋
❋ HEAD TO TOE IN MOSCHINO,
MUMMY LOOKS A DREAM. ❋

✳ HEY DIDDLE DIDDLE

❋ HEY DIDDLE DIDDLE,
THE SKIRT FITS MY MIDDLE, ❋
❋ MUMMY IS OVER THE MOON.
GIORGIO LAUGHED, ❋
"TO SEE HER SIZE HALVED...
SHE'LL BE BACK IN ARMANI SOON!" ❋

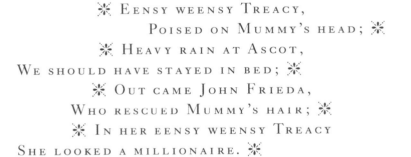

✳ EENSY WEENSY TREACY,
POISED ON MUMMY'S HEAD; ✳
✳ HEAVY RAIN AT ASCOT,
WE SHOULD HAVE STAYED IN BED; ✳
✳ OUT CAME JOHN FRIEDA,
WHO RESCUED MUMMY'S HAIR; ✳
✳ IN HER EENSY WEENSY TREACY
SHE LOOKED A MILLIONAIRE. ✳

❋ HICKORY DICKORY DOCK

❋ HICKORY DICKORY DOCK,
How big is Mummy's rock? ❋
❋ Five carats from Graff,
So we can't pay the staff! ❋
❋ Hickory dickory dock.

 FRÈRE JACQUES

✳ Louis Vuitton, Louis Vuitton,
Mulberry, Mulberry? ✳
✳ Nappy bag dilemma — Lulu, Kate or Anya?
Shopping spree, buy all three. ✳

※ Poor Darling Mummy,
　　　　　Stretch marks on tummy, ※
※ Oh doctor! What can be done?
　　　　　No matter what lotions, ※
※ Or magical potions,
They simply won't tan in the sun. ※

※ Old Mother Hubbard

✳ There was a young woman who lived in her Choos,
Though she once had a house in a smart Chelsea mews. ✳
✳ So much on Jimmy,
The house had to go, ✳
✳ And with it, the Amex and husband in tow!

✳ There was an old woman

✳ PAT-A-CAKE

✳ POP-A-CORK, POP-A-CORK, CHAMPAGNE MAN,
POUR ME A GLASS AS FAST AS YOU CAN. ✳
✳ CRISTAL OR JACQUESSON OR CLOS ST HILAIRE,
AS LONG AS IT'S VINTAGE, I REALLY DON'T CARE! ✳

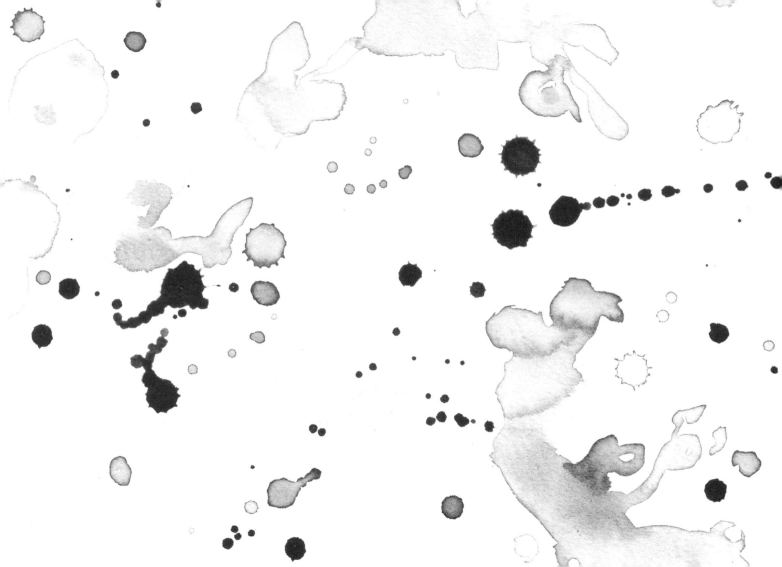

Mr. Christian Louboutin

Thursday, 31st December 3007

@ Home

✳ Cobbler, cobbler

✳ Cobbler cobbler, mend my shoes.
Careful please, they're Christian Lous. ✳
✳ Those red soles, they'll never date,
They'll still be hot in spring '08. ✳

❋ HUSH-A-BYE BABY

❋ HUSH-A-BYE BABY, IN MUMMY'S ARMS,
    WHEN SHE WEARS TOD'S, YOU'LL COME TO NO HARM. ❋
❋ WHEN, IN HER GINAS, SHE'S NOT QUITE SO SOUND,
    YOU'RE SAFER WITH DADDY, BOTH FEET ON THE GROUND. ❋

❋ Pussycat, pussycat

❋ Pussycat, pussycat, where have you been?

I've been to London to visit McQueen. ❋

❋ Pussycat, pussycat, what did you there?

I bought the collection and kissed lots of air. ❋

✳ TWINKLE TWINKLE

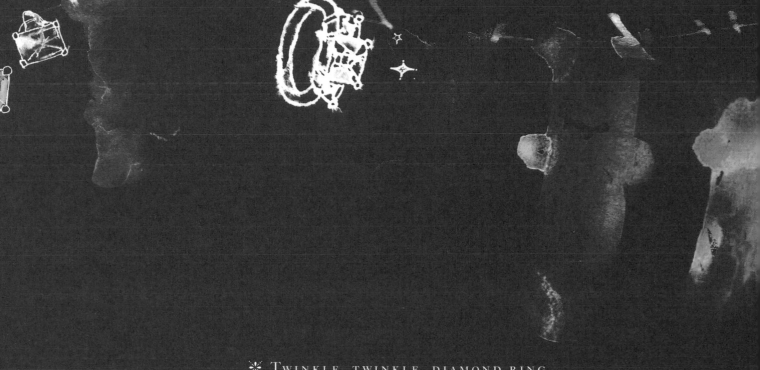

✳ Twinkle, twinkle, diamond ring,
In a blue box tied with string. ✳
✳ Tiffany's new princess cut,
Twice the size of baby's butt. ✳
✳ Twinkle, twinkle, show your spark,
Can't change nappies in the dark. ✳

✳ One, two, three, four, five

✳ One, two, three, four, five —
Hogan trainers in my size. ✳
✳ Six, seven, eight, nine, ten —
Evening dress by Ralph Lauren. ✳
✳ Off to Sloane Avenue,
For Gaultier and Jimmy Choo, ✳
✳ Kenzo and Agnès B,
Design for children, thankfully. ✳

✳ Eenie Meanie

✳ Daddy sweetie, don't say 'no',
Buy an Aston at the show, ✳
✳ If it hurts, the Rolls can go,
Mummy wants a Vantage so. ✳

THE AMANS lie over the ocean,
THE CHIVA-SOM over the sea.
PLEASE pack my CRÈME DE LA MER lotion,
I'M off on a slimming spa spree.

✳

BACK RUBS,
MUD WRAPS,
OH, ring for the masseur for me, for me.
FACIALS,
DETOX,
OH, ring for the butler for me.

✳

I KNOW YOU WANT ice-cream and toy tanks,
I KNOW YOU WANT EURO DISNEY,
BUT MUMMY would rather the GEORGE V,
THE LINEN IS JUST HEAVENLY.

✳

VENDÔME,
FAUBOURG,
LADURÉE'S a haven for me, for me.
LA SUITE,
CRILLON,
LE BRISTOL is pure therapy.

❋ Hush little baby

Hush little baby, don't make a sound,
Papa's gonna give you a thousand pounds.

❋

If a thousand won't buy much,
Papa's gonna give you the Midas touch.

❋

If that Midas touch won't work,
Papa's gonna give you his air-mile perks.

❋

If those perks won't buy first-class,
We'll drink Petrus in some Christofle glass.

❋

If Christofle glass should leak,
At Babington House, we will spend a week.

❋

And if the Cowshed thrills no more,
We'll fly off to Paris for Dior Couture.

❋

If the bill should make Daddy bolt,
We'll raid the diamonds in the Cartier vault.

❋

If the Cartier man is out,
You'll still be the sweetest little baby about!

❋ Baa, Baa

❋ Baa, baa, black goat,
Have you any wool? ❋
❋ Yes, Missoni,
Three bags full; ❋
❋ One for a cami,
And one for a throw, ❋
❋ And one for some cashmere socks
To warm Mimi's toes. ❋

❋ THIS OLD MAN

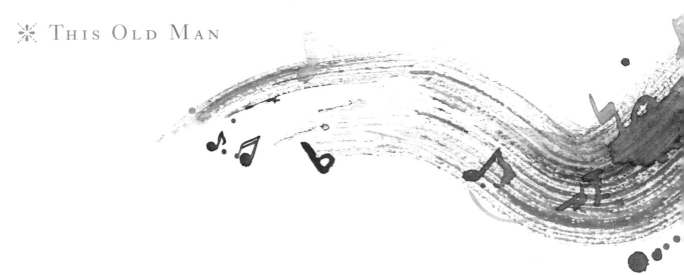

THIS OLD MAN, HE PLAYED ONE,
OFF TO ST TROPEZ FOR SUN,
IN HER GUCCI, PUCCI,
MUMMY NEEDS TO TONE;
TIME TO GET THE TRAINER HOME.

❋

THIS OLD MAN, HE PLAYED TWO,
WAIT-LIST SERGIO ROSSI SHOES,
IN HER GUCCI, PUCCI,
MUMMY'S IN THE KNOW;
PRE-PAID AT HIS AUTUMN SHOW!

THIS OLD MAN, HE PLAYED THREE,
BOND STREET FOR SOME JEWELLERY,
IN MY GUCCI, PUCCI,
SMASH AND GRAB AT FRED;
CAN'T PAY COOK, LET THEM EAT BREAD!

❋

THIS OLD MAN, HE PLAYED FOUR,
BABY'S GONE TO PLAY OUTDOORS,
BEARS IN GUCCI, PUCCI,
BY THE GARDEN PATH;
PICNIC ON MY HERMÈS SCARF.

CONT...

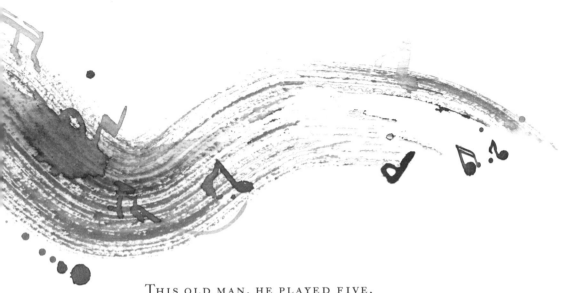

THIS OLD MAN, HE PLAYED FIVE,
ERÈS 'KINI IN MY SIZE,
PACK SOME GUCCI, PUCCI,
IN MY CHANEL TOTE;
CREW OF SIX TO FLOAT THE BOAT.

THIS OLD MAN, HE PLAYED SIX,
LIGHTING DIPTYQUE CANDLESTICKS,
WITH SOME GUCCI, PUCCI,
BABY'S BIRTHDAY TEA;
LET'S SERVE ROMANÉE-CONTI.

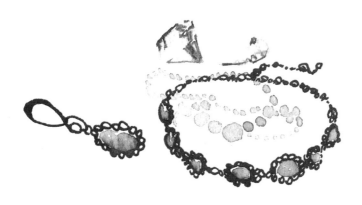

This old man, he played seven,
How I love Capri, it's heaven!
There is Gucci, Pucci,
Even Bulgari!
Big shades à la Kennedy.
✳
This old man, he played eight
Private party at the Tate,
In some Gucci, Pucci,
Gordon made the tarts;
Who comes here to see the art?

This old man, he played nine,
Daddy, buy a diamond mine.
In my Gucci, Pucci,
Something is amiss...
Need some rocks around my wrists.
✳
This old man, he played ten,
Need a month at Chewton Glen.
Dressed in Gucci, Pucci,
Parties round the clock;
Time for Mummy to detox!

ORIGINAL RHYMES

THIS LITTLE PIGGY
First published in 1728

This little piggy went to market,
This little piggy stayed at home,
This little piggy had roast beef,
This little piggy had none,
This little piggy cried "Wee, wee, wee, wee!"
All the way home.

HEY, DIDDLE, DIDDLE
First published in 1765

Hey, diddle, diddle,
The cat and the fiddle,
The cow jumped over the moon.
The little dog laughed
To see such sport,
And the dish ran away with the spoon.

Twinkle, twinkle, little star
First published in 1806

Twinkle, twinkle, little star,
How I wonder what you are.
Up above the world so high,
Like a diamond in the sky.

When the blazing sun is gone,
When he nothing shines upon,
Then you show your little light,
Twinkle, twinkle, all the night.

Pussycat, pussycat, where have you been?
Inspired by one of Elizabeth I's ladies-in-waiting, 16th Century

Pussycat, pussycat, where have you been?
I've been to London to visit the Queen.
Pussycat, pussycat, what did you there?
I frightened a little mouse under her chair.

Eenie meanie minie mo
Late 19th Century

Eenie meanie minie mo,
Catch a Tigger by the toe.
If he hollers, let him go,
Eenie meanie minie mo.

Hush-a-bye, baby, in the tree top
First published in 1765

Hush-a-bye, baby, in the tree top.
When the wind blows, the cradle will rock;
When the bough breaks, the cradle will fall,
And down will come baby, cradle and all.

If you're happy and you know it
Exact origins unknown

If you're happy and you know it,
Clap your hands;
If you're happy and you know it,
Clap your hands;
If you're happy and you know it,
And you really want to show it,
If you're happy and you know it,
Clap your hands.

Baa, baa, black sheep
First published in 1744

Baa, baa, black sheep,
Have you any wool?
Yes sir, yes sir,
Three bags full;
One for the master,
And one for the dame,
And one for the little boy
Who lives down the lane.

I had a little nut tree
16th Century

I had a little nut tree, nothing would it bear
But a silver nutmeg and a golden pear.
The King of Spain's daughter came to visit me,
And all for the sake of my little nut tree.

FRÈRE JACQUES, FRÈRE JACQUES
17TH CENTURY

FRÈRE JACQUES, FRÈRE JACQUES,
DORMEZ-VOUS? DORMEZ-VOUS?
SONNEZ LES MATINES. SONNEZ LES MATINES.
DIN, DIN, DON. DIN, DIN, DON.

HICKORY, DICKORY, DOCK
FIRST PUBLISHED IN 1744

HICKORY, DICKORY, DOCK,
THE MOUSE RAN UP THE CLOCK.
THE CLOCK STRUCK ONE,
THE MOUSE RAN DOWN!
HICKORY, DICKORY, DOCK.

One, two, three, four, five
First published in 1888

One, two, three, four, five —
Once I caught a fish alive.
Six, seven, eight, nine, ten —
Then I let it go again.
Why did I let it go?
Because it bit my finger so.
Which finger did it bite?
This little finger on the right.

Cobbler, cobbler
Exact origins unknown

Cobbler, cobbler, mend my shoe.
Get it done by half past two.
Half past two is much too late!
Get it done by half past eight.

MY BONNIE LIES OVER THE OCEAN
NORTHERN AMERICA, 17TH CENTURY

MY BONNIE LIES OVER THE OCEAN,
MY BONNIE LIES OVER THE SEA.
MY BONNIE LIES OVER THE OCEAN,
PLEASE BRING BACK MY BONNIE TO ME.
OH, BRING BACK MY BONNIE TO ME, TO ME.

BRING BACK,
BRING BACK,
OH, BRING BACK MY BONNIE TO ME, TO ME.
BRING BACK,
BRING BACK,
OH, BRING BACK MY BONNIE TO ME.

LAST NIGHT AS I SLEPT ON MY PILLOW,
LAST NIGHT AS I SLEPT ON MY BED,
LAST NIGHT AS I SLEPT ON MY PILLOW,
I DREAMT THAT MY BONNIE WAS DEAD.
BRING BACK,
BRING BACK,
OH, BRING BACK MY BONNIE TO ME, TO ME.
BRING BACK,
BRING BACK,
OH, BRING BACK MY BONNIE TO ME.

EENSY WEENSY SPIDER
EXACT ORIGINS UNKNOWN

EENSY WEENSY SPIDER,
CLIMBED UP THE WATER SPOUT;
DOWN CAME THE RAIN,
AND WASHED POOR EENSY OUT;
OUT CAME THE SUN,
AND DRIED UP ALL THE RAIN;
AND EENSY WEENSY SPIDER,
CLIMBED UP THE SPOUT AGAIN.

THERE WAS AN OLD WOMAN WHO LIVED IN A SHOE
ENGLAND, 17TH CENTURY

THERE WAS AN OLD WOMAN WHO LIVED IN A SHOE.
SHE HAD SO MANY CHILDREN, SHE DIDN'T KNOW WHAT TO DO.
SHE GAVE THEM SOME BROTH,
WITHOUT ANY BREAD,
AND SHE WHIPPED THEM ALL SOUNDLY, AND SENT THEM TO BED.

HUSH, LITTLE BABY
Early American

Hush, little baby, don't say a word,
Mama's gonna buy you a mockin'bird;

If that mockin'bird don't sing,
Mama's gonna buy you a diamond ring;

If that diamond ring turns brass,
Mama's gonna buy you a looking glass;

If that looking glass gets broke,
Mama's gonna buy you a billy goat;

If that billy goat don't pull,
Mama's gonna buy you a cart and mule;

If that cart and mule turn over,
Mama's gonna buy you a dog named Rover;

If that dog named Rover won't bark,
Mama's gonna buy you a horse and cart;

If that horse and cart fall down,
Then you'll be the sweetest little baby in town.

Row, row, row your boat
Exact origins unknown

Row, row, row your boat
Gently down the stream.
Merrily, merrily, merrily, merrily,
Life is but a dream.

Pat-a-cake, pat-a-cake
First published in 1698

Pat-a-cake, pat-a-cake, baker's man,
Bake me a cake as fast as you can.
Roll it, and prick it, and mark it with a 'B'
And put it in the oven for baby and me.

Old Mother Hubbard
16th Century

Old Mother Hubbard,
Went to the cupboard,
To fetch her poor dog a bone;
But when she came there,
The cupboard was bare,
And so the poor dog had none.

This old man
Exact origins unknown

This old man, he played one,
He played knick knack with his thumb,
With a knick knack, paddy whack,
Give the dog a bone,
This old man came rolling home.

This old man, he played two,
He played knick knack with my shoe,
With a knick knack, paddy whack,
Give the dog a bone;
This old man came rolling home.

This old man, he played three,
He played knick knack on my knee,
With a knick knack, paddy whack,
Give the dog a bone,
This old man came rolling home.

This old man, he played four,
He played knick knack at my door,
With a knick knack, paddy whack,
Give the dog a bone,
This old man came rolling home.

This old man, he played five,
He played knick knack, jazz and jive,
With a knick knack, paddy whack,
Give the dog a bone,
This old man came rolling home.

This old man, he played six,
He played knick knack with his sticks,
With a knick knack, paddy whack,
Give the dog a bone,
This old man came rolling home.

This old man, he played seven,
He played knick knack with his pen,
With a knick knack, paddy whack,
Give the dog a bone,
This old man came rolling home.

This old man, he played eight,
He played knick knack on my gate,
With a knick knack, paddy whack,
Give the dog a bone,
This old man came rolling home.

This old man, he played nine,
He played knick knack, rise and shine,
With a knick knack, paddy whack,
Give the dog a bone,
This old man came rolling home.

This old man, he played ten,
He played knick knack in my den,
With a knick knack, paddy whack,
Give the dog a bone,
This old man came rolling home.

AMY ALLEN

AMY ALLEN IS A FIRST-TIME WRITER AND A FIRST-TIME MOTHER. AFTER GRADUATING FROM OXFORD UNIVERSITY WITH A DEGREE IN JAPANESE, AMY SPENT TOO LONG WORKING IN ADVERTISING AND FOR OTHER PEOPLE IN TOKYO AND LONDON; SHE NOW LIVES MOST OF THE YEAR IN SINGAPORE AND SPENDS THE REST OF THE TIME ON AN AIRPLANE. HER INABILITY TO RELATE TO PEASE PUDDING, HOT OR COLD, AND HER HORROR OF DISNEY-CHARACTER TRAINING CUPS INSPIRED THE REWRITING OF THESE NURSERY RHYMES.

EUN-KYUNG KANG (AKA ZEBBY)

SINCE GRADUATING IN FASHION AND GRAPHICS IN KOREA AND FASHION PROMOTION MEDIA PATHWAY FROM LONDON COLLEGE OF FASHION, EUN-KYUNG'S CAREER HAS CAREENED BETWEEN HER PENCHANT FOR FORTUNE AND HER LOVE OF GRAPHICS. AFTER STINTS AS AN ASSISTANT FASHION DESIGNER, FREELANCE COLUMNIST AND GUEST EDITOR, ZEBBY IS CURRENTLY DEVOTING HERSELF TO ILLUSTRATING. SHE CONTRIBUTES TO AN ARRAY OF MAGAZINES, FROM STYLE BIBLE VOGUE AND I-D, TO THE ARTY AND ESOTERIC NAKED PUNCH.

ZEBBY WORKS WITH INDIAN INK AND WATERCOLOURS, SOMETIMES ESCHEWING BRUSHES AND PENS IN FAVOUR OF CHOPSTICKS. SHE ALSO ASSEMBLES COLLAGES IN PHOTOSHOP.

The charity

Donation

For every copy sold, Spy Publishing will donate 10 per cent of the profit to Save the Children. All donations to this charity help to make a lasting difference to children in the UK and around the world.